For we are God's workmanship,

created in Christ Jesus to do good works

which God prepared in advance for us to do.

Ephesians 2:10

All Scripture quotations, unless otherwise indicated, are taken from the HOLY
BIBLE, NEW INTERNATIONAL READER'S VERSION ®. Copyright © 1995,
1996, 1998 by International Bible Society. Used by permission of Zondervan.
All Rights Reserved.

Published by Scholastic Inc., 90 Old Sherman Turnpike, Danbury, Connecticut 06816

ISBN: 0-7172-7888-3

Printed in the U.S.A.

First Scholastic printing, July 2005

LORD of the BEANS

Written by
Phil Vischer

Illustrated by
Rob Corley, Tom Bancroft,
and Jon Conkling

SCHOLASTIC INC.
New York   Toronto   London   Auckland   Sydney
Mexico City   New Delhi   Hong Kong   Buenos Aires

Toto Baggypants couldn't wait. After weeks of planning, Uncle Billboy's birthday party had arrived! All the Flobbits were there. But best of all, Randalf was there—and he brought fireworks!

"Oooh…aaaah," the Flobbits cried as Randalf's fireworks lit up the night. Even more amazing was the giant birthday cake that sprang from the ground. The Flobbits crowded around the cake, cheering for Uncle Billboy. But where was he?

"Uncle Billboy, I brought you some cake!" Toto said as he walked into Billboy's fancy Flobbit Hole. But his uncle wasn't home. Instead he found Randalf sitting at a table, looking at a small bean.

"Your uncle isn't here," Randalf said. "He had to go. But he left you this bean."

Toto was confused. "Why would I want a bean?" he asked.

"This is no ordinary bean," Randalf said.

"This bean made that cake grow out of the ground. It will give you almost anything you ask for. And it's yours now, Toto."

Toto was worried. "What if I use it wrong? I don't think I want it. You take it, Randalf!"

"The bean is your gift," Randalf replied. "We can't choose what gifts we're given. Only how we use them."

Then Randalf smiled. "I've invited some friends to help you, Toto."

"Meet fearless ranger, Ear-a-Corn, sharp-shooting elf, Leg-o-Lamb, and Grumpy, the gruff but lovable dwarf. They'll take you to the Elders of the Razzberry Forest, who will tell you more about your bean!"

"Can my brother come?" Leg-o-Lamb asked. "He's another elf." So the "other elf" joined the group.

Randalf smiled proudly. "I give you—the Fellowship of the Bean!"

"Got any waffles?" Grumpy said as he stomped off into the kitchen.

This is going to be a weird trip, Toto thought to himself.

The next day the Fellowship of the Bean hiked deep into the Razzberry Forest. Grumpy's stomach grumbled. "Hey Toto," he said, "how about using that bean to make me a chicken burrito?"

"I don't want to use it until I know what it's for," Toto replied.

Grumpy shrugged. "Man, if I had a great gift like that, I'd be using it to get <u>rich</u>! After I made a few chicken burritos."

Toto was confused. Is that what his gift was for?

Toto looked around. "Where are the Elders? All I see is trees!"

"The Elders are the trees," Randalf said. Toto looked around as the great trees opened their eyes and stared down at him!

"Welcome, Randalf," said the tallest tree in a voice as old as Earth.

Randalf showed the Elders the bean. "What should Toto do with it?"

"Take the bean through the Blue Gate into the Land of Woe," they replied. "There he will find his answer."

The Land of Woe? That doesn't sound very nice,
Toto thought.

The travelers said good-bye to the Elders and walked on through the forest.

On and on they walked, until they came to a stone wall.

"Where are we?" Ear-a-Corn asked. Then he noticed a large blue door in the wall.

"The Blue Gate!" he cried. "We found it!"

They opened the door and found a smaller door. It was so small only Toto could fit through. He would have to go on alone.

"You don't have to go, Toto," Randalf said. "The Land of Woe is a terrible place!"

"I want to know what my gift is for," Toto said. "Push me through."

Toto slid through the hole. "That's one brave Flobbit," Randalf said.

Leg-o-Lamb sighed. "We didn't help Toto very much."

Then a man rode by on a bicycle, carrying a large umbrella. He told them about the Red Gate just a few miles down the road. "It's bigger," he said. "But be careful! An angry band of Sporks is nearby. They're looking for a small Flobbit with a bean."

What are Sporks, you ask? Terrible, mean creatures made by the evil Scaryman. Half spoon, half fork—they were his utensils, and they did his bidding!

And now they were after Toto and the bean!

Toto was in terrible danger. Randalf and the others had to stop the Sporks before they found their Flobbit friend!

On the other side of the wall, Toto glanced around. "This place is creepy!" he said.

He sat down by a tree to rest. Toto stared at the bean. "What a lot of trouble you've turned out to be."

Just then something big fell from the tree and landed next to him. Thud! Toto jumped. The "something" was really a "someone" —a strange creature with tattered clothes!

"Who are you?!" Toto cried.

The stranger stared at the bean. "IT'S MY PRECIOUS!" he howled. "They stole it from me!"

The creature jumped for the bean, but Toto was too fast. He grabbed the bean and ran.

Luckily for Toto, the creature was in terrible shape!

"You are pretty speedy," he groaned. "But these woods are tricky! You need a guide, no?"

Toto looked around. He had no idea where he was. Maybe he did need a guide.

"What's your name?" Toto asked.

"I am named for the sound I make with my throat," he said. "Ahem."

Toto was surprised. "Your name is 'Ahem'?"
"Yes, my name is Ahem!" he said.

"I haven't always looked like this," Ahem explained. "I used to be a normal Flobbit until I found that bean. I loved that bean. It gave me all the food I ever wanted—and I didn't even have to work for it."

Toto wondered if Ahem had become so lazy and dirty because he didn't have to work for anything. This couldn't be what his gift was for, could it?

Soon Toto and Ahem arrived at a small village. The land was dry and brown. The people looked very sad and very, very hungry.

"Welcome to the Land of Woe," Ahem said.

Yikes! thought Toto. These people need help!

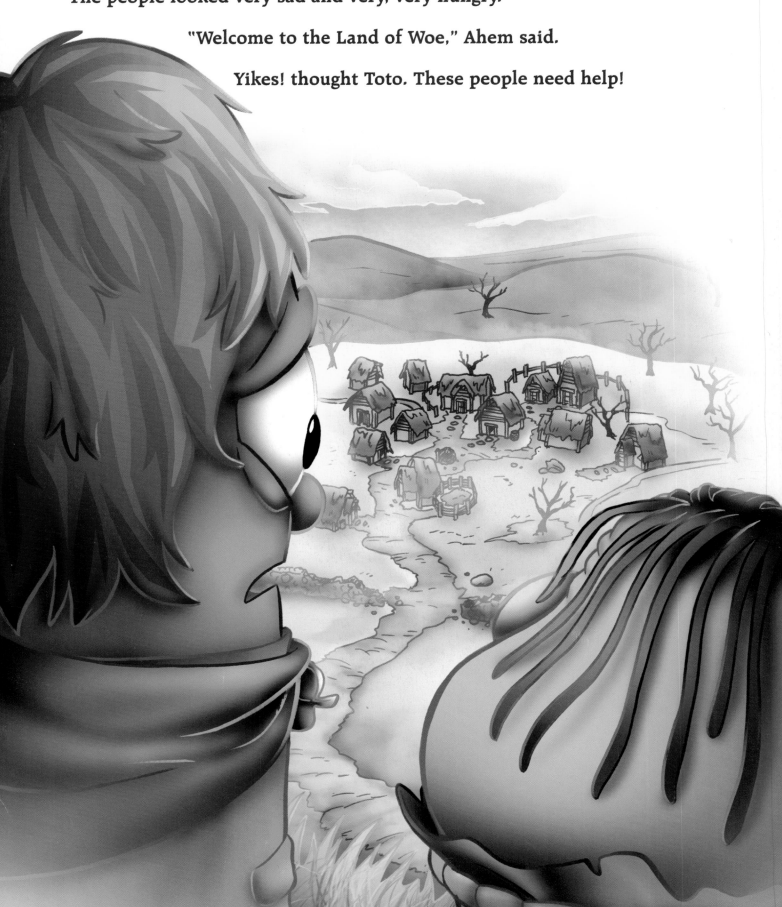

Meanwhile, Toto's friends had found the Red Gate—and the Sporks!

"We can stop them!" Leg-o-Lamb said.

"For Toto!" Randalf cried, and they ran out to face—

—more Sporks than they could even count!

"This is not good," Leg-o-Lamb said. "We're surrounded!"

Then one of the Sporks lifted his nose to the air.
"Something smells yummy," he said.

"Who wants a cookie?"

It was the "other elf" with a plate full of cookies he had baked in the hollow tree. The Sporks happily crowded around the cookies. Leg-o-Lamb's brother had saved the day!

Toto's friends hurried to the village, where they found Toto.

"I know why the Elders sent me here," Toto said. "My gift can help these people!"

"You're right, Toto," said a voice Toto knew very well. It was Uncle Billboy! "Your gift was meant to help people. That's what all our gifts are for."

Excitedly, Toto threw the bean into the dried-up well. Water shot up like a fountain. Now the villagers would be able to grow food again!

Everyone crowded around Toto and cheered. Knowing his gift would help others made Toto the happiest of them all!

Who's Who?

Match the characters from the Lord of the Beans
with the Veggie friends on the next page.

Uncle Billboy

Ear-a-Corn

Leg-o-Lamb

Other Elf

Toto Baggypants

Scaryman

Ahem

Grumpy

Randalf

Jerry Gourd

Mr. Nezzer

Junior Asparagus

Archibald Asparagus

Mr. Lunt

Jimmy Gourd

Pa Grape

The Scallion who has
never been given a name

Larry the Cucumber

Veggie Value to Share

Think of the gifts that God has given to you.
Can you use them to help others, just like Toto?